JANE KEMP and **CLARE WALTERS** have worked together as
a writing team for many years. They are co-authors of several children's books,
as well as a number of books for parents, many of which have been published
internationally. They have also been scriptwriters for the highly successful
BBC children's television series *Balamory*. Jane and Clare formerly worked
on the respected babycare publication *Practical Parenting* and still write
for several magazines. Their previous books for Frances Lincoln are
Dad Mine, Mum Mine, Cat, Dog and *Time to Say I Love You*.

JONATHAN LANGLEY studied at Liverpool College of Art and
Central School of Art and Design. A hugely successful author and illustrator
for children, his books have sold over a million copies throughout the world.
His first book for Frances Lincoln was *Missing!,* which was followed by *Shine,*
written by his wife, Karen Langley. He lives with his family in Cumbria.

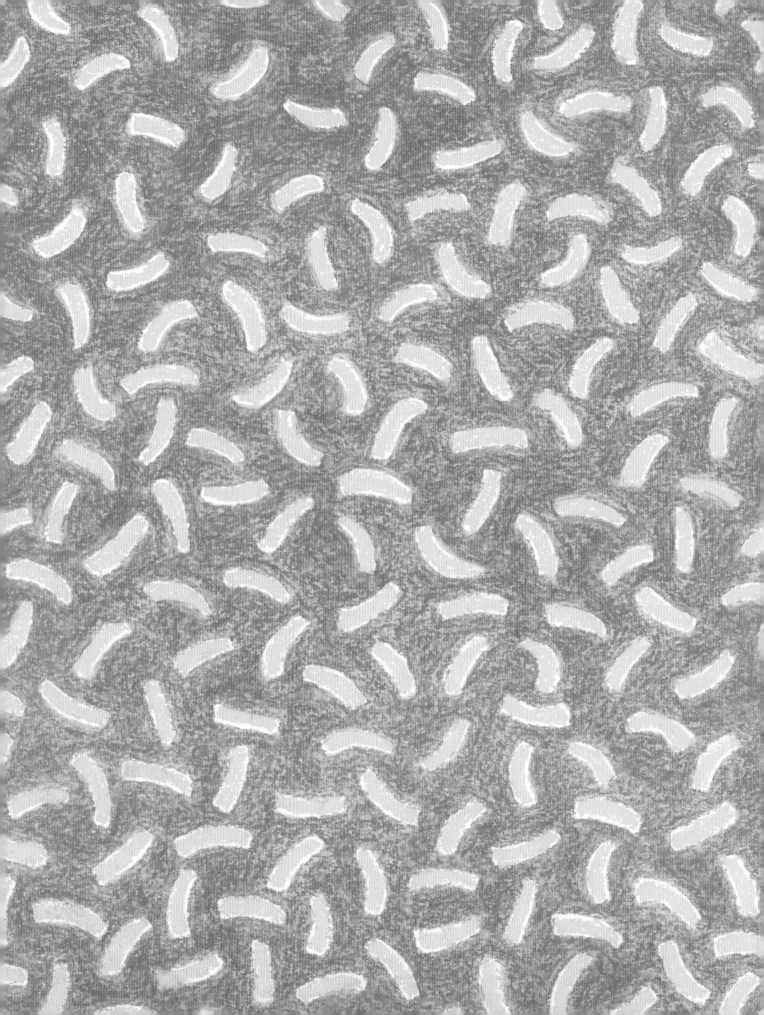

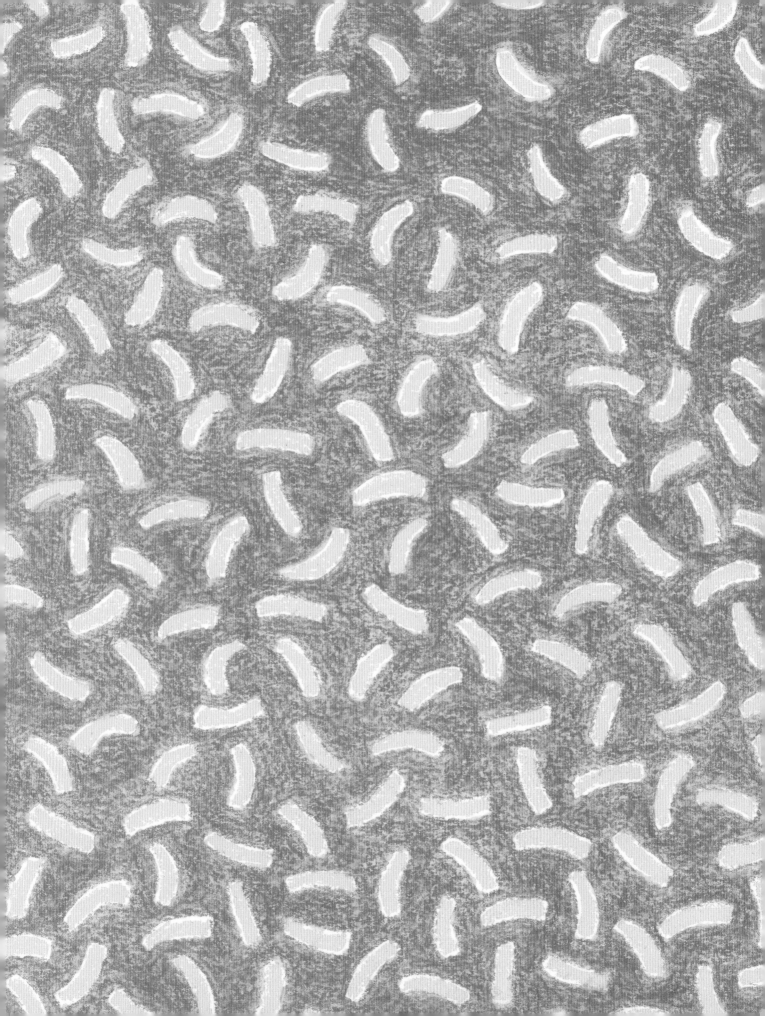

For George, Ralph, Annabel and Madeleine – J.K.

For Alex and Matthew – C.W.

For the children of Levens Church of England School, Cumbria – J.L.

Jane Kemp and Clare Walters

I Very Really Miss You

Illustrated by Jonathan Langley

F

FRANCES LINCOLN
CHILDREN'S BOOKS

Today's a special day. Today's the day
my big brother Ben is going away...

on a school trip
to an adventure camp...

for one whole week!

And I'm GLAD!

Because that means
for one whole week
Ben won't be able to...

So now I can just forget about Ben...

and have a nice time on my own.

But it's a bit quiet without Ben around.
Perhaps he wasn't so bad.

After all, he did...

give me rides,

make funny faces,

pull me up,

and help me clean up
my half of our room.

Mum said, "Why don't you send
Ben a postcard? I'll help you."

So I did. And this is what I wrote:

dear Ben,
   come home soon.
I very really miss you.
love from
   Sam x

Today's a special day.

Today's the day my big brother Ben
comes back from his school trip.
I'm going to meet him.

I try to stay cool. But when I see him getting off the bus...

I can't stop myself. I run and run.

And then I hug and hug him. He gives me
such a *squeeze* I can hardly breathe.

And then he whispers so only I can hear,

"Hey Sam, I very really missed you too."

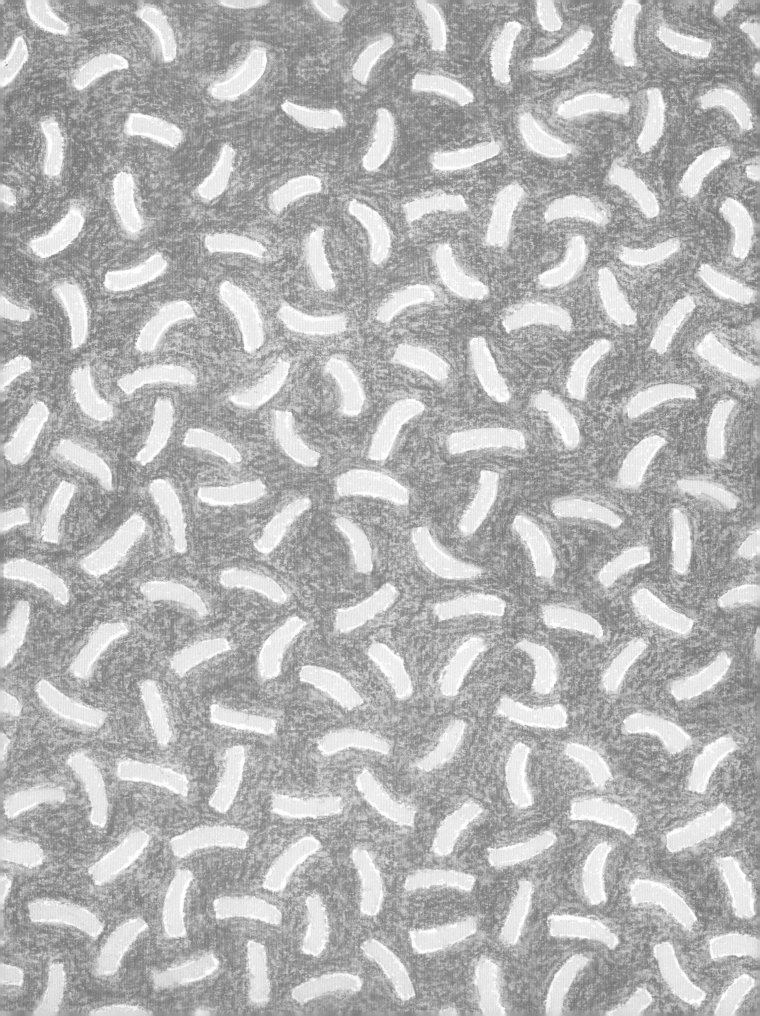

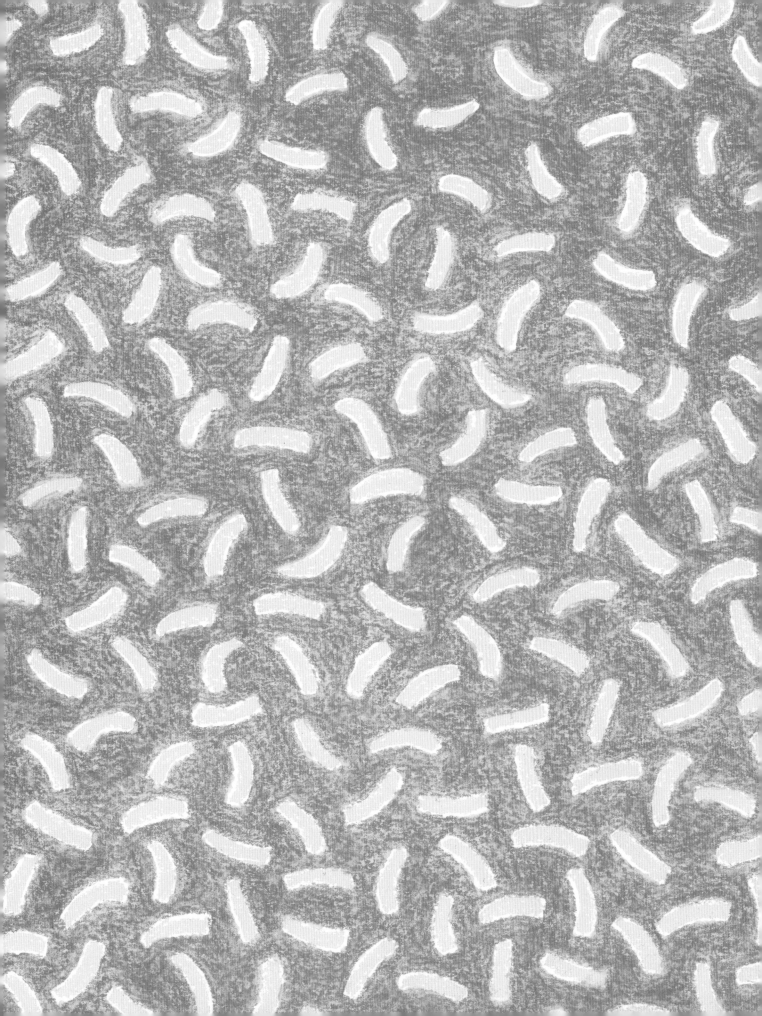

MORE TITLES FROM
FRANCES LINCOLN CHILDREN'S BOOKS

Shine

Karen and Jonathan Langley

Jimmy is very excited – he's a star in the school play! He practises
shining every day and soon begins to sparkle. The night of the
show arrives and it's just about to begin, but Jimmy's dad is nowhere
to be seen! Will he make it from work in time to see
Jimmy's glittering performance?

ISBN 978-0-7112-2116-1

Missing!

Jonathan Langley

Every day, Lupin the cat is there to meet Daisy when she comes
home from nursery. On the first day of the holidays, Lupin waits
for Daisy as usual, but Daisy doesn't appear.
"Where is Daisy?" asks Lupin.
"Where are you, Lupin?" calls Daisy.
And they set out to search for each other.

ISBN 978-0-7112-1543-6

Time to say I Love You

Jane Kemp and Clare Walters
Illustrated by Penny Dale

When is the best time to say I love you?
Shall I say it when you wake me with a kiss?
Shall I say it when we're chasing waves across the sand?
Explore sweeping landscapes and starry skies as a mother chooses
the perfect time to tell her little girl how much she loves her.

ISBN 978-1-84507-449-4

Frances Lincoln titles are available from all good bookshops.
You can also buy books and find out more about your favourite titles,
authors and illustrators on our website: www.franceslincoln.com